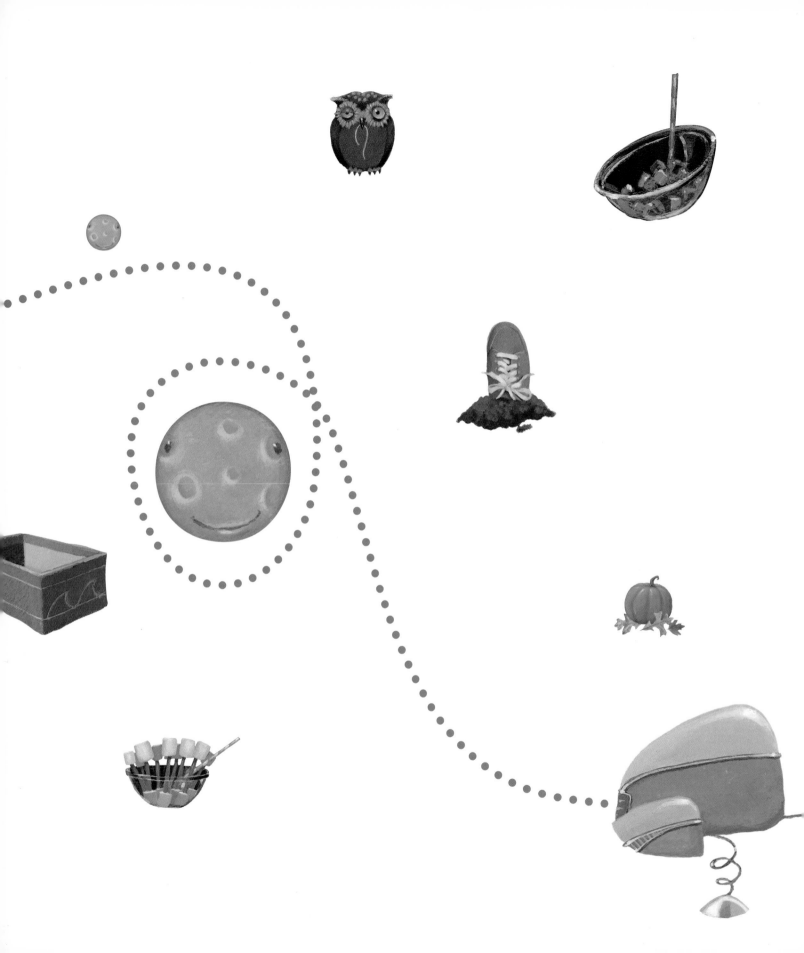

George Hogglesberry

Grade School Alien

by Sarah Wilson
illustrated by Chad Cameron

Tricycle Press
Berkeley / Toronto

Library of Congress Cataloging-in-Publication Data

Wilson, Sarah.
    George Hogglesberry : grade school alien / by Sarah Wilson ;
with illustrations by Chad Cameron.
            p. cm.
Summary: George Hogglesberry, the new second grade student
from the planet Frollop II, gets help from his teacher and classmates
with fitting in and with his performance in the fall school play.
    ISBN 1-58246-063-9
    [1. Extraterrestrial beings--Fiction. 2. Schools--Fiction. 3.
Self-confidence--Fiction. 4. Theater--Fiction.] I. Cameron, Chad, ill.
II. Title.
    PZ7.W6986 Ge 2002
    [E]--dc21
                                                    2001008026

First Tricycle Press printing, 2002
Printed in Singapore
1 2 3 4 5 6 — 06 05 04 03 02

Tricycle Press
a little division of Ten Speed Press
P.O. Box 7123
Berkeley, California 94707
www.tenspeed.com

Book design by EUDESCO/San Francisco
Typeset in Bolbody, DIN Neuzeit Grotesk, Thesis Serif, and Utopia

Before George Hogglesberry went into his new class, he put a nose on his face.

Everyone else had a nose. George wanted one too.

"It's scary being new," he told his parents. "I hope they like me."

Right away, it was clear that George
wasn't from the neighborhood.
"I'm from up there," he said,
pointing at the floor.

"No, down there," he said, pointing at the ceiling.

The words weren't coming out right.

"I'm not sure what's up and what's down," he said. "Come to my house at night and I'll show you."

Miss Skootch's class went on a field trip to George's house.

It wasn't hard to find.

Mrs. Hogglesberry had just planted shoes along the driveway.

"I'm not sure if they'll grow or not," she told Miss Skootch. "I've never had a knack for gardening."

The class looked through a telescope on the Hogglesberrys' roof.

George pointed to a white dot in the sky. "There it is! There's my old school!" he shouted. Suddenly, George felt like there were ice cubes in his stomach. He never had to worry about people liking him up there.

"It's a star!" someone said.

"No," said Mr. Hogglesberry.

"It's Frollop II. It's home!"

"Kind of sends shivers up your elbows, doesn't it?" said Mrs. Hogglesberry.

Everyone looked at their elbows.

"Do you have television up there?" asked Martha MacMillan.

"Sure," said George. "Sort of."

"And root beer? And baseball cards?" asked Warren Harvey.

George nodded. "Something like them," he said. That was all the class wanted to know.

Whew!

George's mother served green beans with marshmallows. "Drink up!" she said.

"Remember that it's hard to be in a new school," Miss Skootch told the class the next day. "Let's try to help George get used to things."

This was no easy job.

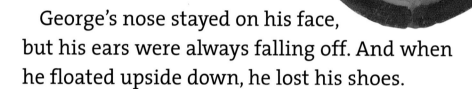

George's nose stayed on his face, but his ears were always falling off. And when he floated upside down, he lost his shoes.

He didn't understand colors at all.

Uh-oh.

He had to be reminded not to walk on the ceiling during recess.

Ooops! I'm sorry.

And he had terrible problems with the drinking fountain.

Help!

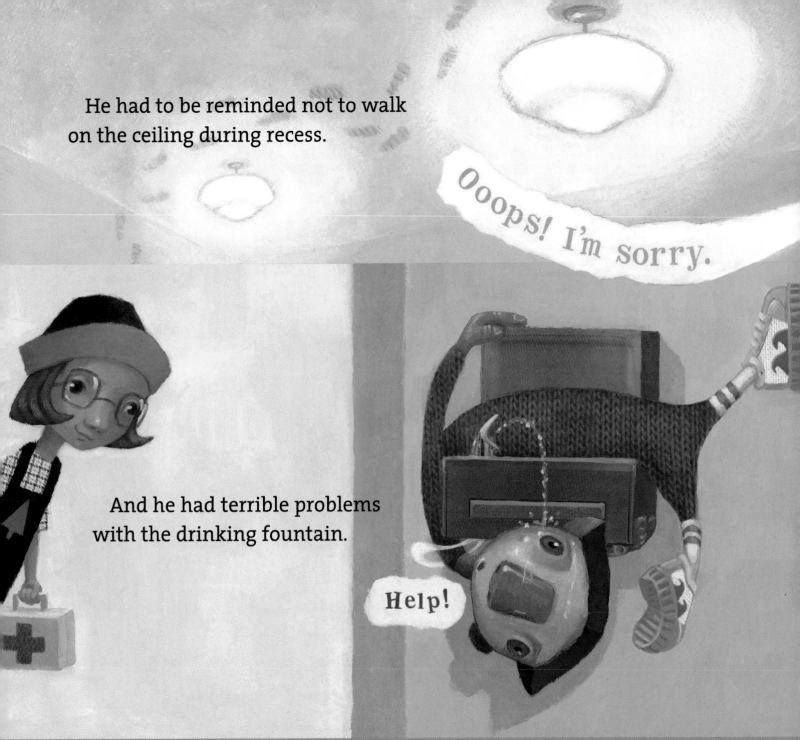

Things weren't going well at all. He was sure everyone was laughing at him, even though they weren't.

Worst of all, no one ever knew who or where George was going to be. Not even George.

Although he was helpful and tried hard to pay attention, sometimes he daydreamed and forgot where he was.

Without meaning to, he'd turn himself into a tomato.

Or an overhead light.

Ulp!

Whoops!

Or even the clock in the principal's office.

This presented a problem when it was time to plan the fall play.

What part would be best for George? And could he stay in it?

"I can be a great volcano!" he told Miss Skootch.

"Hmmm," she said. "I don't think we'll need any volcanoes."

"How about a French-fried onion?" George asked hopefully.

"I don't think we'll need those, either," said Miss Skootch. "Our fall play is usually about dancing leaves. And squash. And pumpkins. Maybe you can be a leaf, George."

"I'll do my best," George promised.

The class worried that he might forget his part and still turn into a volcano or an onion, but everyone helped him practice.

George painted his own leaf costume. Dancing was hard for him, though. He kept floating off the stage and losing his place.

Then one day he blew out of a window.

This was so discouraging that he felt something wet falling out of his eyes.

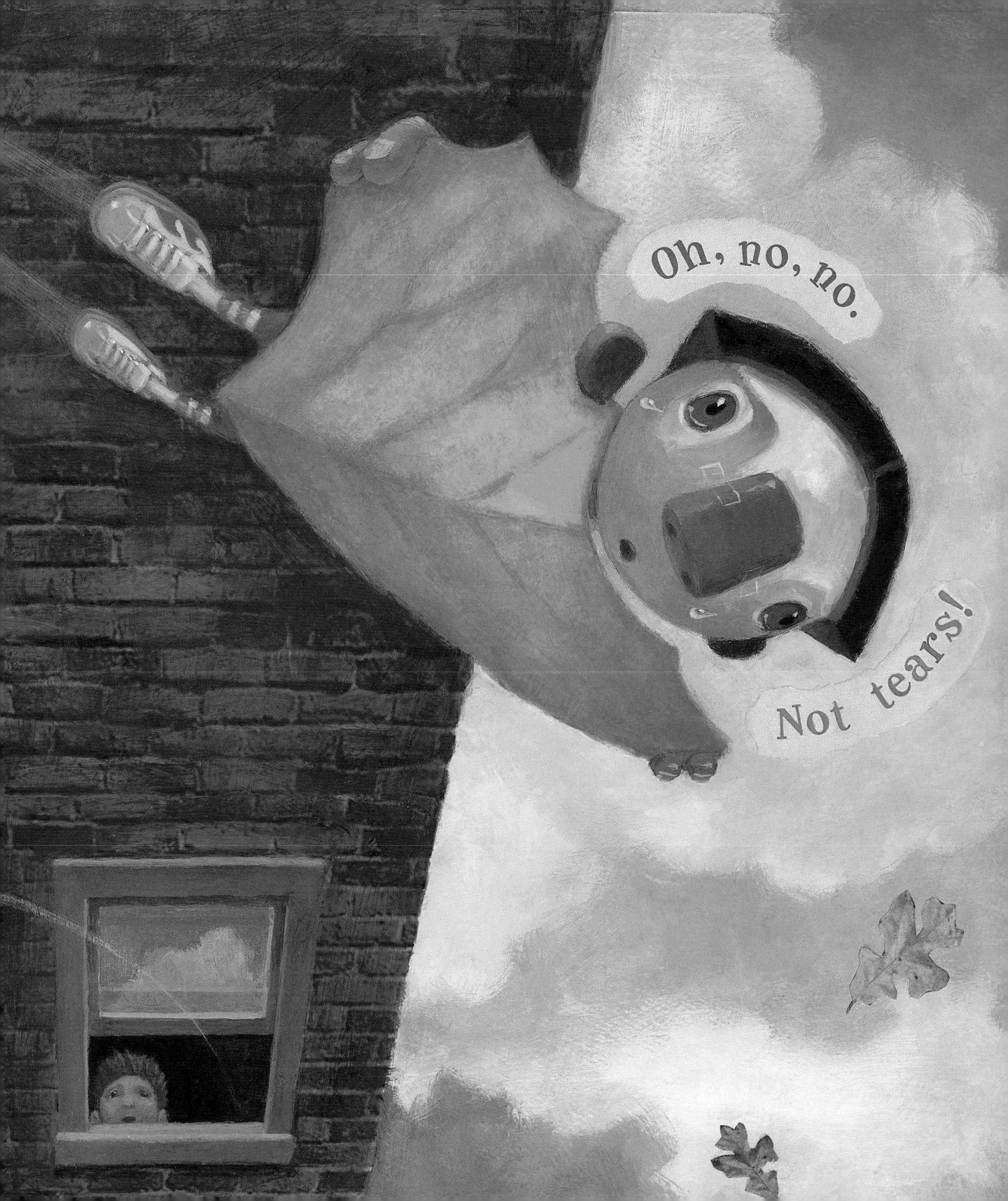
Oh, no, no.
Not tears!

George hid on a bulletin board.

"I'm sure we can find another part for you," said Miss Skootch, gently pulling him off. "Let's give it another try."

George tried to be a squash and then a pumpkin. But those didn't work, either. Everybody thought and thought. There had to be a part for him in the fall play.

Then George had an idea. But he was too shy to say it out loud. He whispered it to Miss Skootch, who smiled.

"I think George has found the perfect part," she told the class.

"But he wants to surprise you!"

On the night of the fall play, George was so scared that his hair turned purple. He'd practiced all week at home for his surprise.

Ellie Barber hugged him. "Just try not to drop your nose or ears or something," she reminded George.

She was trying to be kind, but her words scared him even more. Whenever he thought about the play, his feet lifted off the ground into somersaults.

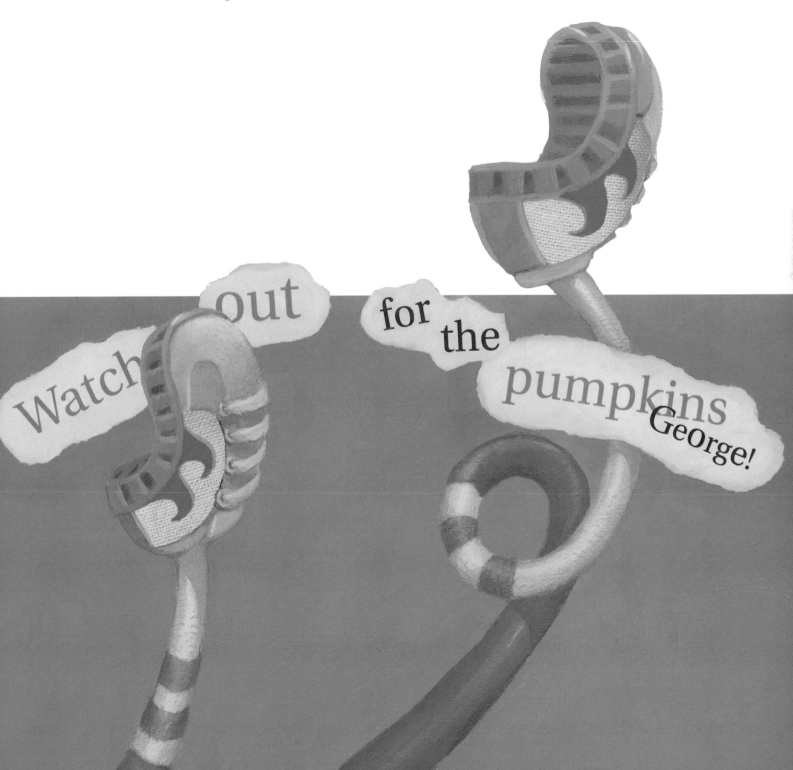

Watch out for the pumpkins George!

Out in front, George's parents were excited. They had dressed up for the evening and sat in the first row. Mrs. Hogglesberry wore toothbrushes in her hair. Mr. Hogglesberry wore a new green mustache. He'd made it himself out of lettuce leaves.

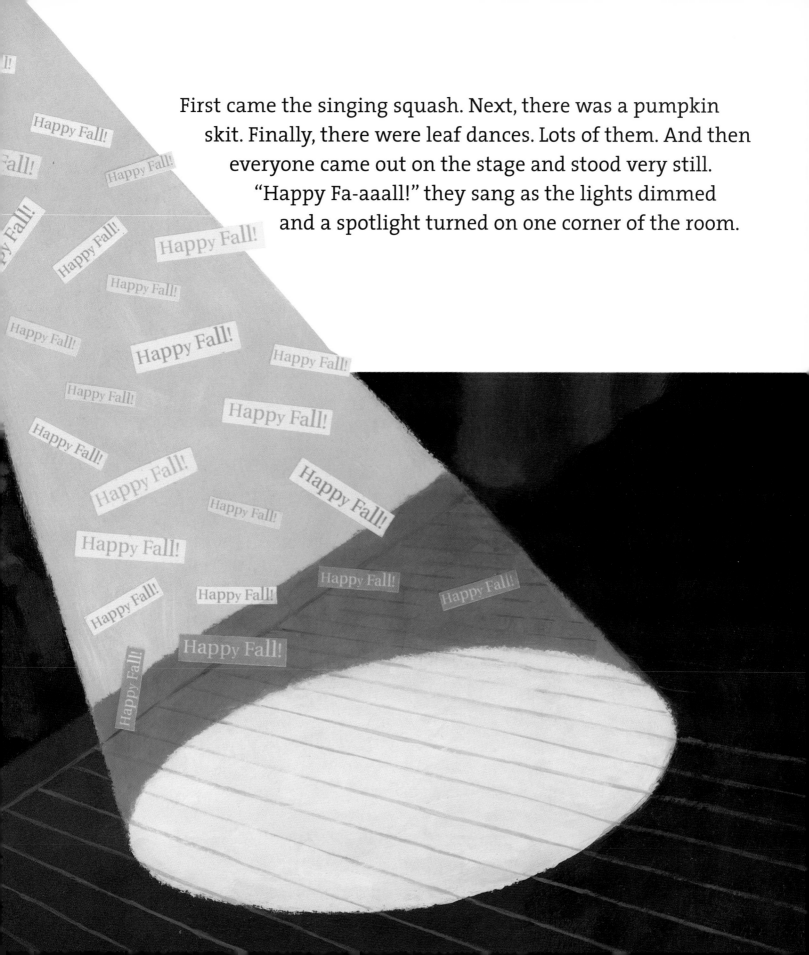

First came the singing squash. Next, there was a pumpkin skit. Finally, there were leaf dances. Lots of them. And then everyone came out on the stage and stood very still. "Happy Fa-aaall!" they sang as the lights dimmed and a spotlight turned on one corner of the room.

There was George Hogglesberry in a harvest moon costume.
"Is it *really* a costume?" wondered Martha MacMillan.
I'm going to be sick, George thought.
Instead, he began to glow brighter and brighter,
and grow larger and larger, rounder and rounder.

So far, so good... so far, so good...

Then—oh, no! He started to

s p u t t e r.

And **spark.**

And **sizzle.**

Was he going to turn into a
French-fried onion after all?
Right there in front of everybody?

The whole class stood frozen on the stage.
What could they do? How could they help him?
Martha MacMillan blew him a kiss and closed
her eyes. Miss Skootch crossed her fingers.

aaaaaaahhhhhhhhhhhhhhhh

Aaa?

But George was only warming up. The sparking and sputtering stopped as he grew even rounder and brighter. His harvest moon was huge now. And beautiful!

"Lovely," sighed Miss Skootch.

George floated gracefully up a wall, across the ceiling, and down to the front of the stage. He lit up the room.

"Happy fall, everyone," he said, bowing. "Goodnight."

There was a moment of silence, and then the whole audience stood up and clapped and cheered. George's moon was a great success!

"We knew you could do it!" shouted the Hogglesberrys.

He was so relieved that he rolled into a small rubber ball and bounced offstage.

"We're all so pleased to have George with us this year,"
Miss Skootch told the Hogglesberrys later. "He brings so much to
the class."

"He says he still falls apart sometimes," said George's mother,
adjusting her ears. "But then, I guess we all do, don't we?"

The Hogglesberrys stayed to drink a few bowls of Jell-O.

When they finally walked home, George was so happy that it was hard for him to keep both feet on the sidewalk.

"I wasn't sure I'd like this new school," he said, "but I do. A lot!"

"You certainly fit in!" said his parents, throwing spaghetti in the yard for the birds.

"We're very proud of you!" The words lit up George's ears.

He slept soundly that night and dreamed of orange Hogglesberry moons, floating bowls of Jell-O, and a sky full of friendly stars. In the dream, Miss Skootch drifted by and smiled at him. Martha MacMillan blew kisses. "Welcome to our planet!" sang his class.

George knew in his toes that everything was going to be okay.

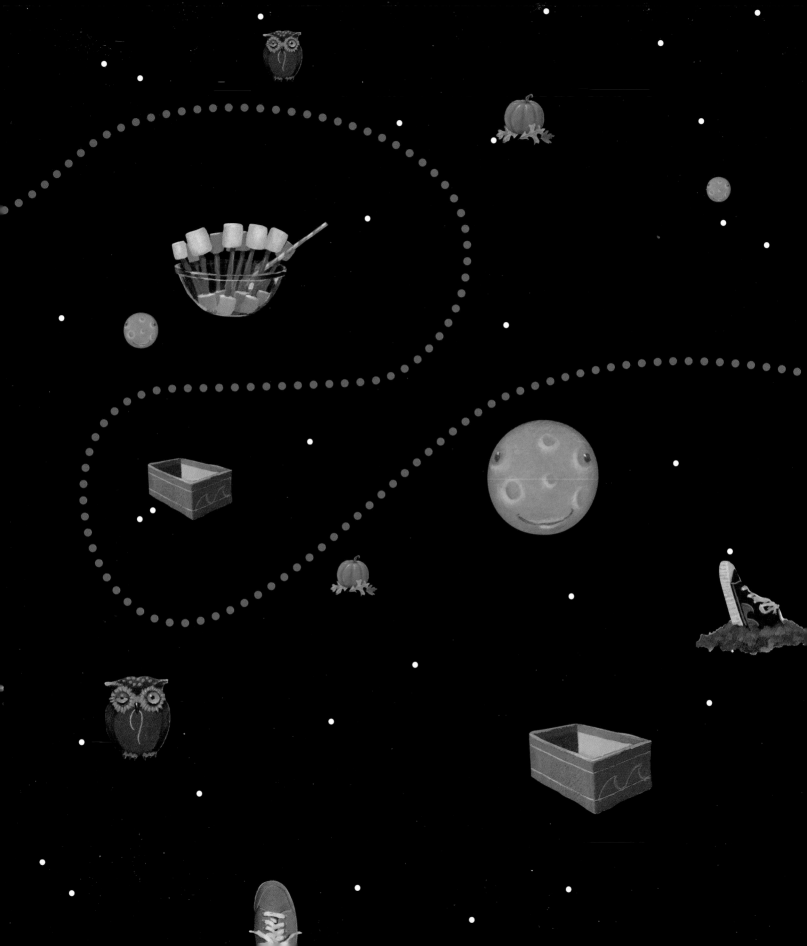